TINY TREE
CHILDREN'S BOOKS

First Published 2021

Tiny Tree Children's Books (an imprint of Matthew James Publishing Ltd)

Unit 46, Goyt Mill, Marple, Stockport SK6 7HX

www.tinytreebooks.co.uk

ISBN: 978-1-910265-94-9

Illustrations by Howard Gray

Japanese text provided by Hideaki Matsuya 松矢英晶

Setsuko loved the sea.

10% of the net profits from the sale of each book will go to the Marine Conservation Society, the UK charity working for seas full of life.
www.mcsuk.org

proudly supporting

She swam its shallows.

She dived its depths.

あまのせつ子は
うみがだいすきでした

One day, when she was swimming far from shore, a shadow filled the sea.

まわりのうみが
くろいかげでおおわれました

The beat of Setsuko's heart rippled
through the water around her.

It was an enormous whale.

たった一とうのくじらが
やってきました

"Don't be scared," he said, "I'm just looking for my friends. I'm so small and the ocean is so big. Sometimes I wonder if I am the last whale."

It was hard to imagine something so big feeling small. But Setsuko understood.

でもせっ子には
わかりました

"My friends have chosen a life on land. You might feel small, but I can see you have a big heart," she said. "Stay here and rest with me. I'd love to play with you."

For a week, Setsuko and the whale shared the sea. He showed her how to make rainbows from sea spray.

せつ子とくじらは
いっしょにあそびました

She told him stories about the fish that used to play hide and seek with her in the seaweed forests and how her friends used to come to share the cold excitement of the sea and dive with her.

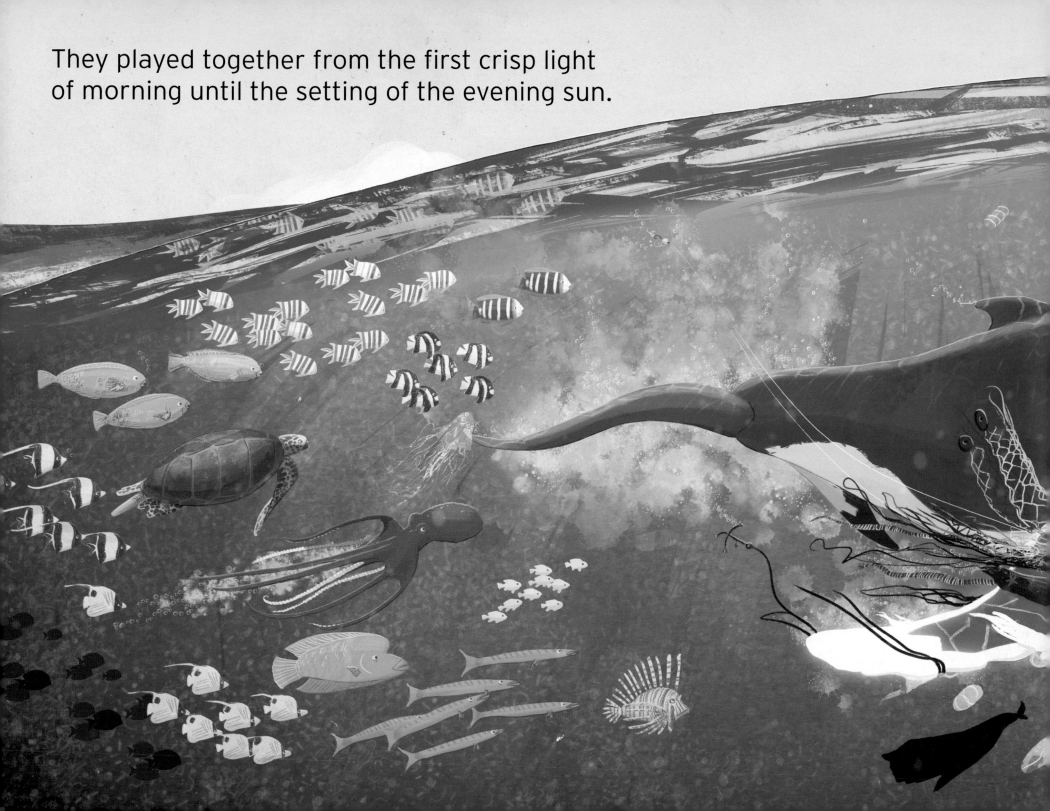

They played together from the first crisp light
of morning until the setting of the evening sun.

ひがのぼり　そして
しずみました

Towards the end of the week, when he thought she wasn't looking, Setsuko noticed the whale looking out into deeper waters.

くじらさん、ひがしへむかっておよぐのよ

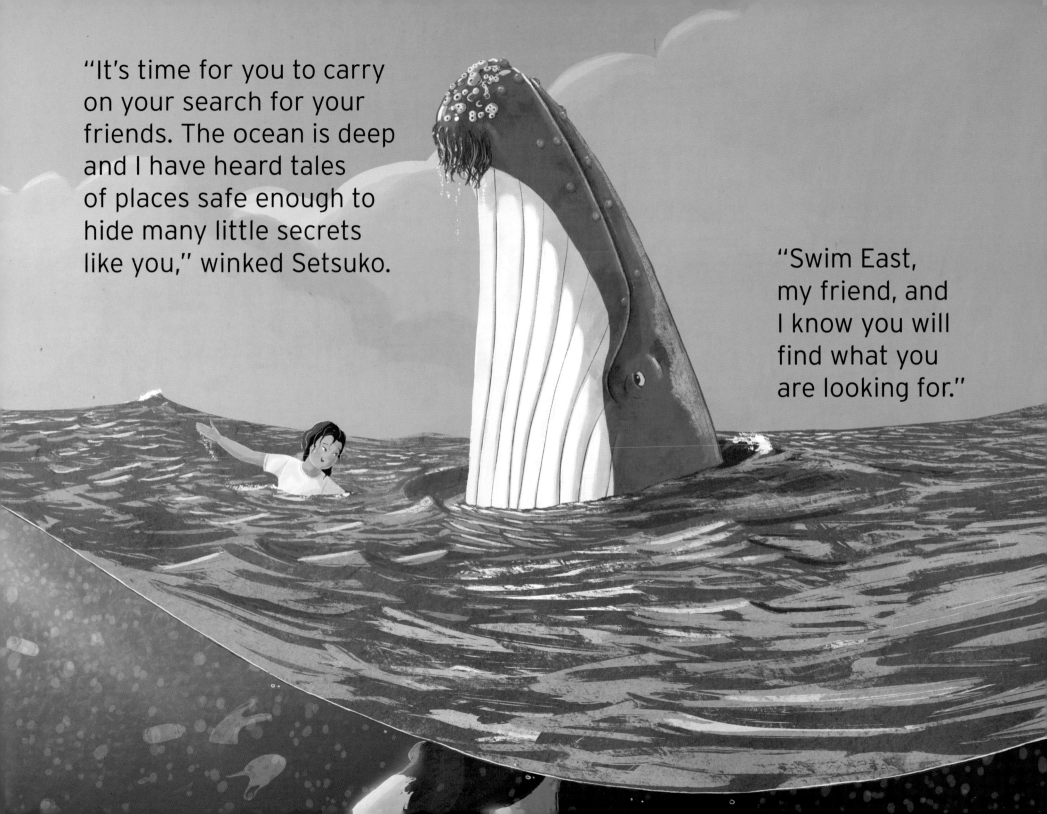

"It's time for you to carry on your search for your friends. The ocean is deep and I have heard tales of places safe enough to hide many little secrets like you," winked Setsuko.

"Swim East, my friend, and I know you will find what you are looking for."

The whale smiled.

"Thank you. You have given me hope; a great gift. Let me give you something in return."

きぼう、それは一ばんのおくりもの

And he began to sing.

The song filled the sea. The song filled Setsuko.
It came to her through the water. She was in the
song and the song was in her. It was the saddest,
most beautiful thing she had ever heard.

うみがうたで
いっぱいになりました

The whale turned to swim towards the rising sun and disappeared into the depths. He had left, but the song remained.

くじらは
とおざかっていきました

Setsuko took the song and made it her own.

せっ子はうみのふしぎとおもしろくもしさについてうたいました

Everyone who heard Setsuko's song was filled with the wonder of the sea. They remembered the beauty and mystery of the ocean.

With the song in their hearts, they asked Setsuko what they must do.

なにをすればよいのか
だれもがしっていました

Setsuko loved the sea.

She swam its shallows.

She dived its depths.

Sometimes, just sometimes, Setsuko thought
she heard the song of the whale once again.

But when she listened carefully there were many voices,
all sending their sweet sound across the swell of the sea.

たくさんのこえがうつくしいおとに
なってうみをわたってくるのです

For Kes, Keston and everyone working
to make the world a better place for them.